Puffin Nibbles

No Cat – and That's That!

Bruce Dawe

Illustrated by **Andrew McLean**

Puffin Books

PUFFIN BOOKS

UK | USA | Canada | Ireland | Australia
India | New Zealand | South Africa | China

Penguin Random House Australia is part of the Penguin Random House group of
companies whose addresses can be found at global.penguinrandomhouse.com.

First published by Penguin Books Australia in 2002
This edition published by Puffin Books, an imprint of
Penguin Random House Australia Pty Ltd, in 2019

Design by Melissa Fraser and Tony Palmer
© Penguin Random House Australia Pty Ltd
Typeset in New Century School Book by
Post Pre-press Group, Brisbane, Queensland

Printed and bound in Australia by Griffin Press, part of Ovato, an accredited
ISO AS/NZS 14001 Environmental Management Systems printer

 A catalogue record for this
book is available from the
NATIONAL
LIBRARY   National Library of Australia
OF AUSTRALIA

ISBN 978 0 14 330009 0. (Paperback)

Penguin Random House Australia uses papers that are natural and recyclable
products, made from wood grown in sustainable forests. The logging and
manufacture processes are expected to conform to the environmental
regulations of the country of origin.

penguin.com.au

This Puffin Book

belongs to

_____

_____

Tick the Puffin Nibbles **you** have read!

 BAD BUSTER
Sofie Laguna
Illustrated by Leigh Hobbs

 FIRST FRIEND
Christobel Mattingley
Illustrated by Craig Smith

 MY AMAZING POO PLANT
Moya Simons
Illustrated by Judith Rossell

 NO CAT – AND THAT'S THAT!
Bruce Dawe
Illustrated by Andrew McLean

 THE MERMAID'S TAIL
Raewyn Caisley
Illustrated by Ann James

 TOPSY AND TURVY
Justin D'Ath
Illustrated by Emma Quay

Visit us at puffin.com.au

For Gloria,

who first introduced me to cats,

and to Lara,

who gave Liz and me

our present cat, Prue.

B.D.

In memory of Dinah,

better known as Puss.

A.M.

Chapter One

'No cat and *that's that*!'

That was Dad at breakfast time.

'Yeah yeah yeah,' Sam mumbled into her Korn Pops. When Dad spoke like *that*, you knew he meant it.

But it didn't stop Sam

from wanting a cat just the same.

'Not a big fat one, like Wendy's got, next door,' Sam explained to Mum

after Dad drove off. 'It could be a little teensy one. I'd look after it.'

'You don't know what trouble cats are,' said Mum.

She put some bacon scraps in Sunny's food dish.

'Not like dogs,' she said, giving Sunny a little pat.

Sunny was Sam's big brother's dog. It had lots of hair. And lots of gross habits Sam tried not to think about. As well as fleas. And it slobbered. And barked at night. And other times, too.

'It's a watch dog!' Dad

had said. 'They're *supposed* to bark!' End of discussion.

But Sam kept on wanting a cat (even a kitten would do, she thought). A little kitty.

She was still thinking about it that night. That night, so much was to happen to her.

Chapter Two

That night it really started to rain. Very heavily.

Sam's house had a tin roof, so you could hear the rain, drumming like an army. Sam tried to go to sleep. She kept tossing and turning.

The noise was worse than
Fredbert's dog. Fredbert
was her brother's name.

What a stupid name to give
someone! But Mum had
liked it. She explained that
it gave her boy a choice –

two names in one, like a
two-flavoured ice-cream!
(Everybody always
chuckled at that.)

Through the rain, Sam
could hear Sunny flopping
around, getting settled in
the laundry and going *woof*!
every so often. Then she
heard another, *different*
sound. A sharp mewing
sound. Out front.

She listened. Yes, there
it was again. It sounded
like . . .

Sam scrambled out of bed.
She could hear Fredbert's

music blending in with the
rain. He always left his CD
player on when he went to
sleep. And that sound *again!*

Carefully Sam eased open

the front door.

At first there was just the rain, like lots of grey pencils slanting down, hitting the leaves of the bushes. Then she saw what she was hoping to see. Something that made her heart do a complete flip-flop!

Chapter Three

A cat. A little, very wet CAT!
A kitten, in fact. Opening
its little pink mouth. Rain
dripping off its whiskers
and fur. It looked up at Sam,
crying for help. What could
she do? She couldn't just
leave it there. Of course not.

Sam picked up the kitten and carried it gently inside. She knew it was a she-cat, of course, because of its pretty little face and its sweet voice.

She crept into her bedroom,
scared someone might see
her. But everyone was
asleep: Dad, Mum, Fredbert,

even Sunny, the dog. The
TV was still on, in the
lounge, but she wasn't
game to turn it off.

In her bedroom she got a
T-shirt out of a drawer and
carefully dried the kitten.

'I'll call you Rainy,' she said, giving the kitten a big hug. Now that it was dry, it was *very* fluffy. And just what Sam wanted!

'You must be tired, you poor thing,' she said.

She cuddled it up in bed.

'Listen to the rain!' she said to the kitten. 'Rainy.' The name sounded good.

But then she started to think about the morning.

What would Dad say?
And Mum? And Fredbert,
who didn't like cats either?
Or Sunny, who *certainly*
didn't like cats?

Maybe she could hide it.
Keep Rainy a secret from
all of them. Having a cat
suddenly seemed (like Mum
said) a lot of trouble!

'Mmorrow . . .' said Rainy, looking up at her with big blue-grey eyes. As if she was saying too: a lot of trouble, coming up fast. How soon, neither Sam nor Rainy really knew!

Chapter Four

Sam must have fallen
asleep then, with the kitten
in her arms, snuggled up to
her flannelette pyjama top.

When Sam woke she got
a terrible fright. Where was
Rainy?

It was still raining so she

wouldn't have gone outside.
But where *was* she?

Sam jumped up. If
anyone else found Rainy,
they'd put her outside in

the street. She had to find
that kitten quickly, or it
would be too late!

The house was in
darkness. Sam couldn't

hear the TV. Someone must have switched it off, after all.

She crept out into the hallway. 'Puss-puss-puss,' she called very softly.

Nothing happened. No Rainy. Then, suddenly, a furry paw touched her bare foot. And a little claw hooked into a leg of her pyjamas! Rainy!

Sam breathed a sigh of

relief. She picked Rainy up
gently. And carried her
quickly back into her
bedroom.

'Naughty little thing,' she whispered. But she gave Rainy a big hug, just the same.

Sam started worrying all over again. About Dad and Mum and Fredbert and Sunny.

Perhaps she could keep her in a cupboard? And feed her with scraps from the table. Like Sunny got.

If she was caught, she could say that she was giving the food to Sunny. But then she'd need milk to drink. Sam remembered the plastic

drink bottle she had taken to
school with her when she
first started.

Then, for the second time
that night, Sam (and Rainy,

too, as far as Sam knew)
drifted off to sleep. Sam
dreamt that she was in a
big jungle with tigers that
all had moustaches like her

Dad did. A jungle full of strange and terrifying sounds. Would she ever be able to escape? No, said the biggest tiger, glaring at her with yellow brown eyes. No NO NO!

Chapter Five

When Sam woke up again, her heart was pumping like mad. What had woken her up? Part of her was still in that jungle. With all those tigers!

What was all that noise? The rain had stopped and

Sam could hear shouts, and running feet. And Sunny the dog woofing away madly.

Sam lay in bed. If I don't get up, it'll go away, be part of my dream, she thought.

Then she had another shock. Rainy had gone again! But where to, this time? She'd be discovered for sure.

'Oh, no!' squeaked Sam.

Now, she just *had* to get out of bed. Even if it meant all her dreams coming unstuck.

She thought of Rainy's
big eyes looking to her
for help.

'I'm coming, Rainy,' she called, as she stumbled into the passageway, 'I'm coming.'

'AND WHERE DO YOU THINK YOU'RE GOING, YOUNG LADY?' said a growly man's voice. Dad!

Sam shook with fright.

'And what's this little *creature* doing in our house?' he asked.

He was holding Rainy by the scruff of the neck, like a pair of smelly sneakers!

Chapter Six

Sam didn't know what to say. This was her worst waking nightmare ever!

'Well, come on, miss!' said Dad. 'Cat got your tongue?'

Mum was standing there, too. And Fredbert, grinning like he was enjoying it.

And that rotten dog, Sunny, who was leaping up, trying to get at the kitten.

Rainy wriggled and meowed in Dad's grip.

'Well, well, come on now. Out with it! This little thing didn't come down with the rain, did it?'

'Yes,' said Mum. 'How *did* it ever get *into* the house?'

'Two guesses,' said Fredbert. 'Somebody who's

always wanted a cat,

remember?'

'Now who could that

possibly be?' said Dad.

All of a sudden Sam
noticed a peculiar smell.

Oh, no! she thought. Don't tell me Rainy's –?

How much worse could things get?

Chapter Seven

'Pup-pup-pup-puplease,
Dad,' said Sam. Her eyes
went all watery. And her
lips felt the way they did
when she got stung by
a green ant last year.

'You've no doubt noticed
that SMELL?' said Dad.

'Y-yes,' said Sam. 'I-I'll clean it up, I promise.'

Then something very strange happened.

Dad's moustache twitched.

'You needn't bother,' he said. 'Fred and I have done that already . . . With a fire extinguisher!'

This was getting stranger and stranger. Then Mum touched Dad's arm and said,

'That's enough, dear. Stop
playing games now.'

Games? Did they think

this was some kind of
game? Why were they being
so horrible?

Dad gave a big sigh.

'That smell, Sam, was the TV going up in smoke. They can, you know, if they're left on all night. And guess who it was that happened to be walking all over Mum and me in bed and woke us up in time? This little visitor!'

He held up Rainy, who wriggled even more.

'Here,' he said, handing the kitten to Sam. 'You'd

better look after her from
now on. And please try
to keep her off our bed!'
Sunny reached for the

kitten, now that she was in
Sam's arms. But to Sam's
surprise, instead of attacking
the kitten, he gave her a lick.

'There,' said Mum. 'You see, we'll have both Sunny *and* Rainy days from now on!'

'And like it!' added Dad.

Sam stood in the passage holding her kitten, and her face was wet. Even though she hadn't been out in the rain!

From Bruce Dawe

I love animals of all kinds. They
are all special in their own ways.
Cats are extra special because they
are so beautiful. When I see kittens
in the pet-shop window, I try to
hurry past because I'd like to take
them *all* home!

From Andrew McLean

I would describe myself as a 'dog person' rather than a 'cat person', so when my wife and three children wanted a cat I pretended I didn't want her (just like the dad in this story). I was determined to be aloof. Dinah, our cat, seemed to sense this and made a point of sitting on *my* lap on most nights for sixteen years. She died this year and I miss her.

Want another nibble?

Being bad was what Buster
did best. Until his dad thought
of a way to sort him out.

Will Adam ever achieve his
dream of being an astronaut?

Becky only wants fairy bread at
her party. But there's so much left
over, and she won't throw it out.

Puffin Nibbles

Scruffy's Day Out

Rachel Flynn

Illustrated by Jocelyn Bell

Dad saves a little scruffy dog
from being run over.
But who does it belong to?

Nicholas Nosh is the littlest pirate
in the world. He's not allowed to go
to sea, and he's bored. Very bored.
'I'll show them,' he says.

Crystal longs to be a mermaid.
So her mother makes her a special
tail. But what will happen when
Crystal wears her tail to bed?

When a bird drops a poo in an empty
plant pot, Emma's mum says that if
she waters it a poo plant might grow!
Could Emma have found the perfect
pet at last?

Puffin Nibbles

First Friend

Christobel Mattingley

Illustrated by Craig Smith

It is Kerry's first day at her new
school. Will she find a friend?

Puffin Nibbles

Topsy and Turvy

Justin D'Ath

Illustrated by **Emma Quay**

Why are Topsy and Turvy so
different? One day they learn why.

Find your story

puffin.com.au